Benjamin Brody's Backyard Bag

WRITTEN BY
Phyllis Vos Wezeman
AND
Colleen Aalsburg Wiessner

ILLUSTRATED BY
Christopher Raschka

BRETHREN PRESS
ELGIN, ILLINOIS

Benjamin Brody's Backyard Bag
Phyllis Vos Wezeman
Colleen Aalsburg Wiessner
Copyright 1991 by Phyllis Vos Wezeman and Colleen Aalsburg Wiessner
faithquest, BRETHREN PRESS, 1451 Dundee Avenue, Elgin, IL 60120
Cover design and illustrations by Christopher Raschka
Library of Congress Cataloging-in-Publication Data
Manufactured in the United States of America
95 94 93 92 91   5 4 3 2 1
Library of Congress Cataloging-in-Publication Data
Wezeman, Phyllis Vos.
Benjamin Brody's backyard bag/Phyllis Vos Wezeman, Colleen Aalsburg Wiessner ; illustrated by Christopher Raschka.
p. cm.
  Summary: Benjamin's playful experiment to find how many things he can do with an empty paper bag leads him to an informative encounter with a bag lady who has no home of her own.
  ISBN 0-87178-091-7
  1. Homeless persons-Fiction. 2. Play-Fiction 3. Imagination-Christopher Raschka, ill. I. Title.
PZ7.W545Be 1991
[E]-dc20
                                  90-39177

DEDICATION

*In loving appreciation of
our parents,*

Margaret June Aalsburg
Joe Theodore Aalsburg

———

Grace Tromp Vos
John Andrew Vos

who gave a special meaning to the
word "home."

Morning was a busy time at the Brody house. The counter was cluttered with bags filled with items the family would need for the bright summer day.

"The sandwiches are ready. I'll put them in your bags," Dad called. He placed a sandwich in his paper-filled briefcase. Another was slipped in between the swimsuit and towel in Tonya's sports bag. The third was perched on top of David's saxophone case. A jar of baby food was nestled into Renee's diaper bag. Into Mom's book bag went the next to the last sandwich on the pile.

"Benjamin," said Dad, "Everyone has a bag but you. Until we can replace your worn-out backpack, we'll have to find another bag for you to use." He reached into the cupboard and pulled out a brown paper shopping bag. It was a nice big one with sturdy handles. He put the sandwich in and handed it to Benjamin.

Benjamin took the bag, and in its emptiness, the
sandwich slid from side to side. He plopped himself
on the step to watch the daily parade as the family
passed by.

His sister, Tonya, went off to swim team practice with her sports bag. The large saxophone case brushed past him as his brother, David, ran off to music lessons. Dad ruffled Benjamin's hair lovingly with the hand that wasn't carrying the brief case.

Mother went to tell Benjamin that they would be going
to the library later in the morning. She found him
sitting on the steps. "What's wrong Benjy?" she asked
when she saw the look on his face.

"Dad's right," Benjamin answered. "Everybody does
have a bag but me. And, everybody's bag is filled
with special things. What can you do with a paper
bag? There's nothing special about it."

"Benjamin, you have a very good imagination. You could come up with lots of ways to use that bag," his mother urged. "It could be just as special as all the others. Why don't you start by filling it with the things you think you will need today?"

Slowly, Benjamin roamed through the house filling up his bag. After a while, he headed for the back yard.

"What can I do with a paper bag," he thought to
himself. A butterfly circled nearby. After a moment he
forgot about his task, and decided to try to catch the
butterfly. He looked for something to use, but the only
thing nearby was his bag. "Maybe it would work," he

said half out loud. Quickly, he emptied the contents of his
bag and ran after the butterfly with sweeping motions.
The bag did work! He caught the butterfly. After
admiring his catch, he watched it fly off once again.

When Benjamin sat down, he realized that he had
found a use for his bag. There must be other things he
could do with it, too. Going through the pile of things
he had emptied onto the grass, Benjamin discovered
the cars he had packed earlier. He laid the bag on its
side to form a garage, and drove the cars in and out of
the opening. He made some obstacles out of the
stones he found nearby. "This is kind of fun!"
Benjamin was beginning to like his bag.

As the cars were returned to the pile, Benjamin picked up a crayon. He used his stones to weight down the corners of his bag. "Maybe I'll keep a list of the ways a bag can be used." Lying on his stomach, he started to write.

When he ran out of ideas, Benjamin found himself staring at the stones. He noticed a sparkle in one, and decided to take a closer look. "I wonder how many kinds of stones there are in my back yard," he thought to himself. It's a good thing I have a bag to hold them."

Benjamin felt hungry, even though it was too early for lunch. The bag would make a good table on which to eat. He placed his sandwich on the brown paper tablecloth. He enjoyed his picnic.

Placing his empty wrapper in the bag, he headed for the garbage can. On the way, Benjamn noticed another piece of paper. "There's another good use for a bag," he discovered as he picked up the paper.

Benjamin's mother was standing on the steps when he returned from the garbage can. He hurried to tell her all the things he had done with his bag. She admired his list and said, "I'm proud of you, Benjamin. Would you like to walk to the library with me? I have a little work to do there. Afterwards
I thought we might stop at a store. Perhaps we can buy you a new backpack for school."
"May I take this bag along?" Benjamin asked. "Maybe I'll find some uses to add to my list. Do you want me to carry anything for you?"
He gathered his treasures, and off they went.

Benjamin carried his bag proudly down the street.
When they got to the mailbox, he reached in and
pulled out the letter he was carrying for his mother.
They passed one of his friends and Benjamin shared a
rock with him. While at the library, Benjamin
entertained Renee by playing games with the bag.
When they left, he put his new library books inside
the bag. They walked through the park on the way to
the store.

As they strolled along, Benjamin became very excited. He pointed to a woman on a bench. She was sorting through a large shopping bag. "Look, Mom, she's playing the game too."

"Maybe she can tell me another way to use my bag," exclaimed Benjamin. "May I talk to her and see?" His Mother thought for a moment. Then she agreed, and they walked towards the woman together.

"Look, I have a bag just like you," Benjamin said to the surprised woman. "I've been playing games with it all day. I'm keeping a list of ways to use my bag. What do you do with yours?"

The woman looked at Benjamin's Mother. She seemed
to be asking if it was OK to talk to the boy. Then the
woman looked at Benjamin. "I use my bag to keep
things in," she told him.

"Oh, you mean like a rock collection?" asked Benjamin.
"I have one in my bag."
"I collect lots of things," the woman answered. "I collect things that people lose or throw away."

"Do you like collections?" Benjamin continued.
The woman took a deep breath. "I need those things
to live. I use my bag to survive. I keep my food and
clothes in it. It holds everything that is important to
me. It holds everything that I own." The woman
looked at her bag and sighed. "This bag is my home."

Benjamin paused. He wasn't sure he understood what she meant. Perhaps for some people a bag was more than a game.

As she shared more of her story, she also shared from her bag. She reached into her treasures and handed him a bright red ball. "You'll have more use for this than I will." She thanked Benjamin for talking to her.

He put the ball into his bag and took out his crayon. He had another use to add to his list. Slowly, he wrote the word "Home."

Benjamin was quiet as they continued their walk. "Mom, when I get my new bag, would it be all right if I kept the old one, too? This one is a lot more special than I thought." "Mom," Benjamin continued, "isn't there a home for her someplace? Or, couldn't we give her a room in our house? I didn't know there was anyone who didn't have a home."

Mother answered gently. "Benjamin, there are many people who do not have a place to live. There are many more people like the woman you met today." "But isn't there anything we can do about it?" Benjamin insisted.

Mother became excited as she thought of a plan. "I think there is," she replied. "Your bag helped you to discover the woman. Now it can help you figure out what to do.

At dinner tonight we can show the family your bag
and the list you made on it. Then we can use the other
side of the bag to make a new list. The new list could
give ways in which we could help."

Benjamin agreed. He started to think of ideas as they walked the rest of the way home. When they arrived at home, the family's bags were piled on the counter again. Benjamin placed his on the top. To him, it was the most special one of all.

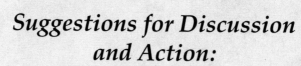

Suggestions for Discussion and Action:

Talk openly and honestly with children about this story and the issue of homelessness. Invite questions and comments while sharing your own thoughts and feelings on the topic. Tell children facts about homelessness without scaring them. Include causes of homelessness, such as mental retardation, loss of home through fire or illness, relocation due to divorce or abuse, unemployment and high housing cost.

Because the causes of homelessness are many, the possibility of multiple and varied responses also exists. Help children to realize that they can do something about homelessness, regardless of their ages.

- Involve them in action so that they do not feel powerless.
- Expose them to people and agencies who are working to combat homelessness or to meet the needs of homeless people.
- Design a specific project to work with a local public, private or church agency. This could include a blanket drive, a coat collection, donations to purchase clothing, contributions of household furnishings, participation in a project to build or renovate housing, or provision of food for homeless centers.
- Become aware of on-going projects to which you can contribute time, money or goods.

A list of additional resources on homelessness is available from faithQuest, Elgin, Illinois